MIND
WRITER

MIND WRITER

STEVE COLE

With illustrations by
Nelson Evergreen

Barrington Stoke

For Simon Wrigley

First published in 2016 in Great Britain by
Barrington Stoke Ltd
18 Walker Street, Edinburgh, EH3 7LP

www.barringtonstoke.co.uk

This story was first published in a different form
in the *Puffin Post* © 2011 Steve Cole

Text © 2016 Steve Cole
Illustrations © 2016 Nelson Evergreen

The moral right of Steve Cole and Nelson Evergreen
to be identified as the author and illustrator of this work
has been asserted in accordance with the Copyright,
Designs and Patents Act, 1988

A CIP catalogue record for this book is available
from the British Library upon request

ISBN: 978-1-78112-583-0

Printed in China by Leo

CONTENTS

CHAPTER 1

Secret

Guess what, world? I can read minds.

Luke Mellows stood rigid on the edge of the playground, well away from the crowds of other kids. Sweating. Alone.

'Guess what else?' he thought. 'It's scaring the hell out of me.'

Luke was used to being able to guess what other people were thinking. It had been that way his whole life. When teachers asked questions, the right answers would just pop into his head. He could make his parents happy by doing what they wanted before they had to ask him. And in sports he knew what moves the other players were going to make before they made them. That was a good way of making the small amount of talent he had go a lot further.

It was all cool. Or it had been.

Before today.

Today Luke seemed to know *exactly* what people were thinking.

It had started with Miss Han this morning. She was writing a task up on the whiteboard when the words crackled across Luke's brain –

'I'm broke. I can't afford the rent. I hate this job ...'

Luke had jumped in surprise. "Too much information!" he yelped.

Everyone swivelled round to stare at him like he was crazy and Miss Han snapped at him to be quiet.

Luke had realised there and then.

He hadn't heard Miss Han speak. He'd heard her *thoughts*. And other thoughts were crowding into his head too. It was as if the rest of the class were thinking aloud, but only he could hear them.

'God, Mellows, you stupid show off.'

'Dad's gonna kill me if I don't get better grades.'

'If he got his hair cut, Luke might be boyfriend material.'

'I am totally bunking off History after break.'

'If I skip lunch again I'll have enough money to buy that game ...'

Luke had put his hands to his ears, jumped up, knocked over a chair and fled from the classroom.

He cringed at the memory. Now Miss Han was going to report him to the Head and his classmates thought he was a freak.

"And I know that for a fact," Luke muttered. "Because I can read their minds ..."

'I'M GONNA HURT SOMEBODY. WHO'S FIRST?'

The thought was like a Rottweiler bite in Luke's brain. He spun round and saw Dan

Stenton swaggering up to him, flanked by his two best buds.

"Oh, great," Luke groaned. Stenton was the biggest kid in Year 10, probably the thickest and definitely the nastiest. But his mates weren't far behind – and their minds were itchy with the promise of seeing a smaller kid take a battering.

'And here I am,' Luke thought, 'standing alone in the corner of the playground. Perfect target.'

"Oi!" Stenton bellowed. "Are you the kid who threw the fit this morning?"

Fame travels fast.

"I'm Luke Mellows."

"What?" Stenton scoffed. "Puke Smellows?"

His mates sniggered. A crowd of onlookers had sniffed blood and was gathering around them, ready for action.

Luke swallowed hard. He'd always been told that if you stood up to bullies they'd back down. But right now, Stenton's thoughts were saying something very different.

'I'm sick of teachers bossing me,' he was thinking. 'I'm gonna take it out on this little –'

"It's not worth it, mate," Luke said. "Beating me up, I mean. The teachers will only give you more hassle."

"What?" Stenton pushed Luke. "Think you're clever, do you?"

The crowd started to chant. "Fight! Fight!" Their sweaty thoughts were like little fists swinging in Luke's head. He felt dizzy and sick.

Stenton grinned. "Puke Smellows, I'm gonna rip your head off and kick it round the playground!"

Luke got ready to run.

"Only ... I can't." Stenton had frozen. "You ... you're tougher than me, Luke. Stronger than me."

Luke blinked in shock. The crowd's chant only lasted a second or two more before it petered out into disappointment.

"You could beat me in a fight, easy," Stenton went on. "You're excellent. I'm nothing."

One of Stenton's mates grabbed his arm. "Duh! You could have him, easy!"

"No." Stenton stood there like a zombie. "Luke Mellows rules. I'm nothing."

Now the crowd was laughing and jeering. What was Stenton playing at? Luke felt uneasy, too. He found himself *trying* to read the bully's mind.

But there was nothing in Dan Stenton's head. No thoughts, no memories, no feelings.

It was like his mind had been wiped clean.

Luke was totally freaked. He stared as Stenton jerked back to life and barged away through the crowd as if he was blind. His mates mooched after him, heads down, scared.

Luke tried to shut out the startled thoughts of the gobstruck crowd as they drifted past him.

'Not fair!'

'What a let-down.'

'Huh. Thought there would be blood.'

'What happened?'

'Stenton's lost it!'

But one girl hung back and watched Luke. She was tall, thin, straight up and down. She had black hair and brown eyes, and was wearing a different school uniform. Luke didn't recognise her, but somehow he felt like he'd known her for ages.

She looked kind of snooty. Crafty.

"I suppose it's a bit like having a satellite dish in your head," the girl said. "You know. The way you pick up signals."

Luke stared. "Huh?"

"I'm talking about your power. Your *gift*."
The girl leaned in and added in a whisper, "You can read people's thoughts. Can't you?"

"What?" A chill bristled up Luke's spine.
"Who are you and how could you know –?"

"Relax," the strange girl said. "My name's Samira and I know you want to keep your power a secret. I *like* secrets – which is why you can't read *my* mind. Can you?"

Luke realised she was right. He couldn't pick up on a single one of Samira's thoughts. "I ... I don't know what you're talking about," he said.
"Get lost."

"It would be a mistake to upset me, Luke."
Samira smiled. "You saw what I did to Stenton."

Luke swallowed hard. He was feeling even more uneasy now. "That was something to do with you?" he asked.

"That was everything to do with me." Samira gave a little laugh. "See, Luke, you might be able to *read* minds. But I can write all over them."

CHAPTER 2

Control

Luke watched as the rest of the students spewed out from the school buildings, choking the drive in the home-time rush. He hung out by the bike sheds, waiting for the swarm of kids to thin.

He didn't want people around him. Way too freaky. Way too hard.

It was as if his mind had become a radio. It picked up the thoughts of anyone close by and played them back to him. And just when it seemed things couldn't get any more weird, he'd met *her*.

Samira, who'd found out about his powers. Samira, who could put thoughts into people's heads.

Samira, the mind-writer.

"You should listen to her," a voice behind him said.

Luke spun round to see Mr Hertzog, the science teacher, standing behind him. His eyes were glazed and his head lolled to one side.

"Uh ... what was that, sir?" Luke asked.

"You should be friends with her," Mr Hertzog said. "Or she'll make life hard for you."

Luke closed his eyes and tried to read the silent chatter of the teacher's thoughts. But there was nothing there.

She was making him say this.

"Samira!" Luke shouted. He stared round wildly. "I know it's you. Where are you?"

After a moment, she sidled into sight from behind the bike shed.

"I didn't like the way our last little chat ended, Luke," she told him. "You ran out on me. It was naughty of you to do that." Her eyes were dark and cold. Her smile was a crooked slit. "So ... I had to tell your teacher."

Luke swallowed hard. "I don't get this. None of it."

"Your powers are new to you. I suppose you're scared." She shrugged. "I was scared too when I learned the truth about our 'accident' – and what I could do to others."

"Accident?" Luke licked his dry lips. "What are you on about?" Again, he tried to read Samira's mind, but there was only a cold, silent darkness behind her eyes.

"Uh-uh. No peeking." Her smile grew crafty. "First I need to know I can trust you."

'Well, I don't trust you a millimetre,' Luke thought, 'and I've had enough of this.' He said nothing, but when he turned to leave Mr Hertzog grabbed him by the arm and twisted tight.

Luke gasped and turned to stare back at Samira. "Stop this," he pleaded.

"I can't." Samira looked shaken for a moment. "It ... it won't let me."

"It?"

The moment passed and the girl's eyes grew hard again. "Now your mind is open, things can start to happen," she said. "This is your last chance to make friends with me and do things the easy way. But don't take my word for it. Listen to a responsible adult."

"Make friends," Mr Hertzog repeated, and a big stupid smile pulled tight across his face. "Make friends with Samira. Do things the easy way ..."

In terror Luke yanked himself free of Mr Hertzog's grip and fled.

'It's not happening,' he thought. 'It can't be happening.'

Luke's breath came in whimpers, and his frantic footsteps jarred through his body. He was panting by the time he reached the end of the school drive, and only then did he risk a look back.

Mr Hertzog had gone. But Samira stood there still. Watching him.

Who is she? How did she know this would happen to me today?

The questions stabbed into Luke's mind, so that they drowned out the thoughts of the people he passed.

'What does she want with me?' he wondered. 'And *what* won't let her stop?'

Luke was drenched with sweat and trembling by the time he made it home. His mum called a cheery "hello" to him as he slammed the front door shut. With a shudder of relief he ran in to join her. At last he felt safe again.

Mum looked up from her computer, and Luke winced as a rush of her thoughts flashed into his mind.

'Good, now I've got an excuse to stop work.'

'Why is he always such a scruff?'

'Hang on, he's pale and sweaty –'

"Been running?" Luke's mum asked out loud.

"Uh ... yeah. Quick kickaround," Luke lied. He backed away a bit. "Mum ... did I ever have an accident when I was little?"

She looked at him in surprise. "Accident?"

Her thoughts were clear as day in Luke's head. 'He can't mean that time at the hospital ...?'

"That time at the hospital," Luke prompted her.

She frowned. "How would you know about that?"

"I ... I heard you and Dad mention it once," Luke said.

"It wasn't an accident," his mum said. "It was when you were tiny. We'd taken you to hospital for a check-up and you had a funny turn, that's all." She smiled, as if it was nothing. But Luke found that her thoughts told a different story. Luke felt her panic, saw a jumble of images of a little boy having a terrible fit. His eyes were all white ... Doctors crowded round with no idea what was going on.

"White eyes," Luke murmured, as he remembered Samira's dark stare.

His mum stood up. "Are you sure nothing's ..." Her head lolled to one side. "Wrong?"

Luke felt her thoughts empty to silence. "Mum?" he said.

"Oh, dear." His mother smiled a blank smile. "You know, she can run just as fast as you can, love."

"She?" Chills ran through Luke as he watched his mum shuffle into the kitchen and stand beside the cooker. "Oh, no. Not you too. Wake up!"

"I wonder what would happen," his mum said with an icy calm, "if I turned on all the gas rings for a while and then lit a match?"

"Mum, stop it!" Luke grabbed her wrist to try to stop her twisting the dial, but she slapped him away. He stepped back, his cheek stinging. The sudden hiss of gas was like snakes – its thick, eggy smell catching in his throat. "You'll kill us," he said. "STOP IT!"

Then he caught sight of movement behind him. Samira was looking in at the kitchen window. Her arms were folded, her eyebrows raised.

Mum held up the matches and smiled as the gas went on hissing. "Are you ready to make friends with Samira now?"

CHAPTER 3

Casket

"So where are we going?" Luke asked.

"You'll see."

Luke felt he'd seen more than enough already. He trailed behind Samira as she strode through the warren of back streets at the edge of town. Now and again she would glance back at him with a look of amused impatience on her face, as if she were walking a naughty pet dog that wouldn't come to heel.

Luke supposed anyone else would do exactly what Samira told them.

'But I can *read* people's thoughts, just as she can write over them,' he thought sullenly.

Somehow the two of them seemed to cancel each other out. Samira couldn't control Luke's mind, and he couldn't peek inside her head.

Stalemate.

"What's the matter, Luke?" Samira's lips were stretched in a smug smile. "Still sad because your mummy tried to kill you?"

"You're sick."

Luke knew that he would never forget the sight of Samira as she watched from the window, working his mum like a puppet on a string. Luke had begged her to let his mum go and she had nodded, smug and satisfied. He'd promised to do anything she wanted.

Mum had stood in front of the hissing cooker and dropped the match with a big, brain-dead smile on her face.

Luke shuddered. The situation was so impossible, so crazy.

So scary.

"Don't worry about your mum," Samira went on. "I made her forget the whole thing. And I told her not to expect you till late." The smug smile sat hard on her face. "Till *very* late."

"I still don't see why you need me," Luke complained as he followed her into a side street. "Your powers are way stronger than mine. What can I do that you –?"

All of a sudden Samira turned and gripped Luke round the throat. She forced him against the wall, into the shadows of the street. He gasped as she pressed her face close to his. Her eyes were black as storm clouds.

"What use is strength if it's not focused?" she said with a snarl. "If *he* is to know true power at last, he needs direction ... *insight*."

"Get off me!" Luke pushed Samira's hand away and shoved her backwards. He gulped for breath. "What are you on about – if *he* is to know true power?"

"You'll see," Samira said. She was smiling now, as if nothing had happened. "We're here."

Luke looked around and saw that the side street led on to a quiet courtyard and a sign.

DARKE CLOSE
REST HOME FOR THE ELDERLY

"Here?" Luke asked. "What, are we going to visit some old farts?"

"There's something I need you to look into." Samira was already ringing the bell. "Or rather, some*body*."

A nurse opened the door. Luke listened in on his humdrum thoughts for a few seconds –

'Haven't stopped all day.'

'Don't recognise this pair.'

'Bit young to be on their own.'

Then a single glare from Samira dammed up those thoughts, turning down the volume on the man's mind. With a blank smile, he moved aside to let them past.

"Shut the door behind us," Samira told him.

The nurse obeyed in silence.

Samira led the way along a maze of dingy corridors. It stank of disinfectant and something much worse underneath. They passed no one. Luke had a sudden feeling that he was in a nightmare. Something terrible was waiting for him here, drawing him closer. His heart thumped, and the hairs rose on the back of his neck.

At last they reached a heavy wooden door. Samira opened it without a sound. The curtains were drawn, the evening sunlight murky behind folds of heavy blue fabric. It was like being underwater.

Luke saw someone lying in the bed, swamped in white sheets. A shrivelled shape, dark-skinned with short white hair. It was a man and he was breathing. Just.

"Well, here we are, Luke." Samira's voice was flat, with no feeling. "This man knows something important. But unfortunately he doesn't care to share it with anyone. So …"

"You want me to read his thoughts?" Luke stared at the tiny old man. "He's, like, a million years old. He probably doesn't have much mind left to read."

"You'll see," Samira said. "You *will* see."

Luke took a nervous step closer to the man in the bed. A single word burst into his head like a firework.

NO.

"Sorry!" Luke was jolted backwards. "I ... I didn't mean to ..."

"What is it?" Samira snapped.

GET OUT.

The words creaked through Luke's senses like rusty hinges on a door that had been blocked off for years.

OUT.

"He ... he won't let me read his thoughts," Luke stammered. "He's strong."

"He's old," Samira hissed. "A relic of a dead time. He can't stop you looking."

OUT.

Luke flinched as the thoughts scraped through him.

HE WILL GET OUT.

"You must look," Samira shouted. "Look deeper."

Luke closed his eyes. A shape was forming in his mind. A small box. Weird symbols were scratched on it, wild and complex.

"I see ... some kind of casket ..."

GET OUT. ESCAPE.

Samira took a step closer. "What's there?" she asked. "Tell me."

The box was growing more and more solid. It was shaking. As if something was trapped inside. Luke felt paralysed with fear.

HE WILL KILL YOU, BOY.

"Tell me what's there!" Samira screamed.

KILL EVERYONE.

"No ..." Luke whispered. "No, I mustn't see –"

The old man's eyelids cracked apart like eggshells. His eyes were as white as ghosts.

And, in Luke's mind, the lid of the casket began to open ...

CHAPTER 4

Demon

The casket's every detail blazed in Luke's mind. Its lid was twitching and trembling.

"Don't let it open!" he shouted. "DON'T!"

The old man jumped up from the bed and shoved Samira aside. With a shout of anger she crashed over a chair and to the floor.

An old, cold hand closed on Luke's. The man's milky white eyes had turned dark.

"Shedim," the old man hissed. Luke thought it must be a name, or a magic word.

And then, in a blink, the room had vanished and Luke and the old man were in a shadowy, creaking space. It was hot and airless. For a confused moment Luke thought the casket had swallowed them up. Its image still lingered in the back of his eyes, like the red ghost of a camera flash. Then he looked around, saw junk and boxes and rafters, smelled age and must and dust.

"Brought us here. Bought us time," the old man muttered. His eyes were wise and brown now. "The quiet space that crowns this ruined building ..."

"The attic," Luke translated.

"I mean my head." Shedim – it *was* the old man's name, Luke could sense that – was rubbing his temples. "You woke my mind with your reading. I had foreseen as much. I set aside enough strength to flee here. But the girl, and the Demon inside her, will find us."

"Demon?" Luke's heart was beating faster and his brain felt ready to burst. "I don't get any of this. How did you even bring us here?"

"A wise man asks questions that matter." Shedim looked at him. "Do you believe there's good in people?"

As Luke stared into Shedim's dark, lined face, his fears dimmed. He nodded.

"There are legends that tell of a magician who summoned demons and learned their secrets," Shedim murmured. "He longed to help all mankind. He walked the world, looked into the hearts of others to learn what they most desired, then granted their wish with his demon magic."

"He read their minds?" Luke said.

"And hated what he found there." Shedim slumped down on an old box. "Such selfish, dreadful hungers. Some longed to bring death upon their enemies ... Some to satisfy their base desires ... Some craved power over others ..."

"But there must have been some nice people with kind wishes –" Luke began.

"So few," Shedim said sadly. "And the Demon had granted the magician powers to help all mankind. The magician could not choose to help certain souls over others – the contract was bound in charms and blood and could not be broken. But one day, the magician thought he'd found the answer. He bargained with that same Demon for the power to put thoughts inside the heads of men. He would *make* them wish for noble things ..."

"The power of a mind-writer," Luke breathed. Now he understood Shedim's words. "So the old magician could read minds like me but also write over them, too – like Samira?"

"Yes." Shedim nodded. "I could."

Luke felt chills zigzag down his backbone. "*You* could? *You* were the magician?"

"Such powers, I had ..." A faint smile played about the old man's mouth. "But the Demon was using me from the start. He grew stronger inside me every time I used his magic. I was arrogant and so I thought I could make mankind better, stronger, by changing dark thoughts to light. But the Demon was plotting the reverse. When he grew strong enough, he planned to turn all good in human minds to evil … and he wanted followers who would glory in his madness." Shedim sighed, looked down. "When I saw at last how my foolishness had fed and fattened my Demon, I fought against him."

Luke nodded. "What did you do?"

"I lacked the skill to kill him," Shedim said. "But I had magic enough to starve him, to make him sleep. I expelled the powers from my body – the power to read minds, *and* the power to bend them – and hid those powers within the bodies of others."

"Others like me and Samira?"

"There have been so many through the ages," Shedim whispered. "Strangers I chose, always in twos, and always ignorant of the powers buried inside. Each time one of the pair dies, the powers are compelled to move into other vessels close by."

Something clicked in Luke's head. "The 'accident' I had at the hospital when I was small," he said. "Mum said my eyes went white. One of your chosen people died there?"

Shedim smiled a sorry smile. "Yes," he said. "And at the same time, the eyes of poor Samira grew shadow-black. But my choice was always wise, Luke. Trust that. You must ... trust ..."

The old man's voice was lost in a long, heavy breath.

Luke felt baffled and afraid. "Shedim, please," he said. "If we're not supposed to know about these powers inside us, how come we do?"

A voice spoke behind him. "Because the Demon has found us, Luke."

It was Samira. The attic door had opened without a sound. She stood now in the doorway, her face lost in shadow.

Luke turned to Shedim. He might be weird and freaky, but he was the grown-up here. The one who knew what was going on.

The one who was slowly slipping to the floor.

Little time left, he'd said.

Samira took a step closer. "All these centuries, Shedim kept his Demon in darkness," she said. "But Shedim is dead now."

'The casket I saw in Shedim's head,' Luke thought, and his panic rose. 'The Demon's prison. Opening.'

"That's right. As the Demon stirred, he reached out to awaken our powers." Samira's eyes were bright and perfect black. "First me. Then you. But the power to read and the power to write were meant to be used as one. And they *will* be, Luke. They will be."

With a hard, wide grin, Samira opened her arms and flew across the dark attic towards him.

CHAPTER 5

Spiral

To Luke it felt like some mad nightmare.

Samira was coming at him. Her eyes were beetle-black, her arms and legs at mad angles, and her face was twisted with longing.

Luke dodged aside as she lunged for him. He started to run, but he tripped over something soft and warm ...

The body of Shedim.

Luke felt a sharp tangle of words spider through his mind – the ancient magician's last, jumbled thoughts.

Stop it – read – her – like a child allowed – read –

Luke rolled clear of Shedim's body. Samira stood over him, a scatter of limbs in the attic shadows.

"Let me wake the Demon in you," she breathed. "Let the mind-reader and the mind-writer be one ..."

Luke looked behind him. A dim line of daylight showed him the doorway. Then Shedim's voice crept again through his thoughts –

"Read yourself, Luke. The answer is there."

'But ... Samira said you were dead!' Luke yelled in his mind. 'I thought you told me to read *her*? What did you mean, *like a child*?'

"The answer is inside you." The hoarse voice was growing impatient. "Read yourself!"

Luke's eyes snapped open. Samira was crouched beside him, her skinny knees pointed at him, the sharp nails of her fingers reaching for his face.

"No!"

Luke pushed her away, scrambled up and ran to the door.

On the other side, wooden stairs spilled downward in a tight spiral. Luke hurtled down the steps, three at a time, and crashed through the door at the bottom, into one of the rest home's dingy corridors.

A nurse came around the corner. "You'll only make her angrier," he said. His voice was calm. "Is that what you want?"

Luke could hear rapid footsteps on the stairs behind him. He bolted forward, barging the nurse aside, and ran on along the corridor until he came to a junction.

Which was the way out?

He picked one way at random – and ran straight into a crowd of elderly patients.

"Do as Samira says," they chanted. They filled the corridor, slack-jawed, vacant.

Luke could only force his way through the zombie scrum. Bony fingers pinched at his arms, his shoulders, his neck.

At last he pushed past the mob and into an empty bedroom. Yellow net curtains flapped at the open window. Luke scrambled up and out into the gardens, gulping down fresh air.

"Read myself?" he panted, trembling. "One word – terrified."

Luke ran on. Soon he came to a wall covered in ivy, and used the thick, woody stems to help him climb. But as he reached the top, he saw a paper boy look his way and skid to a stop on his bike.

"Give up," the boy shouted. He dumped his bike and walked towards Luke with his fists clenched. "Samira will catch you in the end."

'But I don't have to make it easy for her,' Luke thought.

He dropped down from the wall and grabbed the fallen bike. The boy ran after him, but Luke was already pedalling away, adrenaline lending him strength and speed. He wasn't sure what shocked him more – the way he had stolen the bike in broad daylight or the fact he'd actually managed to –

Escape?

As Luke turned into the busy street he realised that cars were screeching through red lights and mounting the pavement, driving straight for him.

"Oh, no way …"

Luke swerved, put on a burst of speed, weaved between two parked cars and bumped up onto the kerb.

There was a hollow slam and an explosion of glass as a truck crashed into the two cars just a second later.

Luke felt sick with terror as he sped down an alley too narrow for cars to follow.

With a start he realised the alley ran alongside the town hospital, where all this had begun. The place was so big, there had to be a quiet place where Luke could hide out and "read" his own mind to find the answer Shedim promised was there.

"I *can* get out of this," he told himself. "I can!"

Luke cycled into the hospital car park and ditched the bike outside the main door. He was panting for breath and his clothes and hair were soaked with sweat as he hurried past Reception, into a maze of corridors.

A sign on a door read STORE ROOM.

Luke checked no one was looking, then ducked inside the small space. It stank of bleach and a light flickered on as soon as he opened the door. It revealed only a stack of cleaning stuff. Luke was dizzy with relief as he shut the door and forced himself to slow his breathing.

To focus.

To peer inside himself. To listen.

"I *can* get out of this," he whispered again.

As he said it, Luke felt something spark deep inside. He frowned and focused, desperate for Shedim's plan to work.

Think. Read your own thoughts. Get the answer.

"I can get out …"

With a start Luke realised it wasn't his own voice he could hear. This was deeper. A growl, cracked with great age.

The image he'd seen before in Shedim's mind blazed into his senses. The dark casket threatening to open.

I can get out of this BODY at last.

"No," Luke whispered.

"*The Demon has found us.*" That was what Samira had said at the old people's home. This nameless creature of the dark had stirred after so many hundreds of years, and had let its hidden powers steal into their minds.

And now, Luke understood what had happened. He had tried to read his own thoughts, and instead he had snooped into those of the Demon buried inside him.

Luke felt sick with dread as he tried to close the lid of the casket in his mind. But all he could see was his reflection in the glass bottles on the shelves before him.

His eyes, glowing white. His smile, splitting wide.

CHAPTER 6

Promise

Luke stared at his gruesome reflection.

The Demon's taking control of me.

Numb, cold blankness spread through Luke's mind. His thoughts no longer sprang clear into his head. He was having to read them as though they belonged to somebody else. It made him feel weird – truly out of his mind.

The door opened behind him and Samira came in. Her black-eyed smile mirrored his own.

"You wanted this all along," Luke whispered. "I mind-read that the Demon longed to be reborn, and you wrote the wish into reality."

"There *is* no you and I any more," Samira purred. "We *are* the Demon. He will devour our wills, and he will take our flesh, and he will shape it into a fitting form."

"A new body at last," Luke rasped, in a deep voice that was not his own. "A single creature of the dark that all shall worship."

"I shall overwrite the thoughts of all with hate and evil," said Samira, in the same voice. "Their pain and rage and despair shall read like poetry."

"No!" Luke fought against the Demon's grip.

Like a drowning man clutching at driftwood, Luke's thoughts had seized on the last thoughts of the ancient magician. Shedim had hoped to starve the Demon by hiding its powers within others – others like Samira, like him.

Stop it – read – her – like a child allowed – read –

"Don't fight any longer." Samira leaned forward and pressed her head against Luke's. "We are one again, at last."

A pulse of cold power flashed through Luke's senses. He groaned with fear and closed his eyes. He felt like a fly wrapped in a blinding white web as the spider's mouth brushed his skin, drawing him in.

'Look,' came the echo of the old man's voice. 'Look inside Samira as I told you. Read her thoughts as a child would read.'

Not *allowed*, Luke realised.

The word was ALOUD.

Samira's clammy face was pressed against Luke's. Her breath was rank in his nostrils, her black eyes a blur. He no longer knew where he stopped and she began. Soon the mind-reader and mind-writer would be united once again.

"Samira," Luke gasped, "if I'm still here, I know you are too. Shedim said he chose us for a reason … That reason must be because we're strong enough to fight the Demon. We *are*."

He doubled up with pain as blackness and brightness did their best to blot out his thoughts, and the store room racks shook and rattled about them.

"The Demon's trying to break me," Luke said. "That might mean he's going easier on you. Let me in, Samira. Let me read *your* thoughts, not his ..."

Samira whimpered. She jerked her head away from Luke's and shut her eyes.

And all of a sudden it was as if Luke could see more clearly. He saw words in her head, bright and large.

"I ... hate ... you," he read. "Don't want to be you ... I will never be you ..."

'Yes, read it out loud,' he told himself. 'Mind-reader is becoming mind-writer! *Use* that ...'

"I hate you," Luke repeated. "Don't want to be you. I will *never* be you ..."

I will get out. The cold Demon voice rang in his ears. *I will get out.*

"No." Slowly, Samira spoke along with Luke. "Your time ... has ... passed."

Luke took strength and hope from Samira as they chanted together. *"Your time has passed."*

It was as Shedim had always planned. The powers that the Demon had longed to take were now being turned against him. Luke felt as if a storm of energy was building and blowing about the room.

"*I* will *get out*," the Demon protested, but now its own voice was the one that was muffled, growing faint and feeble in the roar of the storm. *Get out ...*

"Yes," Samira shouted. "Get out of us."

"GET OUT!" Luke yelled.

The storm rose to its peak as he opened his eyes.

Warm brown eyes, brilliant and unafraid, looked back into his own.

Samira's eyes.

For a moment it was like being blinded by a camera flash. The storm blew itself out. Luke glimpsed a light-dark shadow flitting about his vision, rattling the racks in the store room like a vengeful phantom.

But then Luke's eyes cleared, and the shadow was gone. He checked his reflection – his own tired green eyes looked back at him.

It was over.

"I … I'm sorry." Tears wet Samira's cheeks. "It took me, controlled me. I couldn't fight it like you could."

"I don't think Shedim meant you to," Luke said. "I reckon the Demon could only be destroyed as it was reborn. And Shedim always knew we were a match for it … together."

Samira stared, and her smile was soft and uncertain. "Are we really free of it?"

Suddenly the store room door burst open. A hospital porter glared down at them. "What the …?"

Automatically, Luke tried to read her mind – and found he couldn't.

"Sorry," Samira said. "We were just leaving."

"Yeah," Luke murmured. "Leaving the past behind."

He grabbed Samira by the hand and together they pushed past the porter, down the corridor and out through the hospital Reception, into the evening light. The streets were still busy with people, their thoughts and dreams their own and nobody else's.

Luke and Samira looked at each other for a time. They didn't need special powers to know what the other was thinking.

'The Demon's gone. But we must never, ever meet again. Just in case ...'

A smile passed between them like a promise. Then they let each other go and took their different ways home.

Our books are tested
for children and young people by
children and young people.

Thanks to everyone who consulted on
a manuscript for their time and effort in
helping us to make our books better
for our readers.

If you liked this action-packed thriller, then you'll love ...

An explosive new trilogy from the author of the *Bodyguard* and *Young Samurai* series.

They say you can't
outrun a bullet.
What if you could stop one?

Chris Bradford

BULLET
CATCHER

They say you can't
outrun a bullet.
What if you could stop one?

OUT
NOW

Chris Bradford

BULLET
CATCHER

SNIPER

OUT
NOW

is Bradford

ULLET
TCHER

BLOWBACK

They say you can't
outrun a bullet.
What if you could stop

June
2017

When Troy survives a lethal terrorist attack, he realises
he has a rare skill. He's a bulletcatcher, bullets just
bounce off him. And so he's recruited into SPEAR — a
unit of super-kids on a mission to protect the rich and
powerful of Terminus City. But as the Army of Freedom
scales up the violence, the unit's ability to safeguard the
city — and themselves — is tested to breaking point …